The GOBBLE GOBBLE MOOOOOOO Tractor Book

Jez Alborough

HarperCollins *Children's Books*

The GOBBLE GOBBLE MOOOOOO Tractor Book

Early one morning,
when Farmer Dougal
was still asleep...

Sheep climbed up on to the big red tractor.

'What are you doing?' asked **Cat**.
'I'm going for a ride,' said **Sheep**.
'This is the sound the tractor makes
when you turn the engine on...

'Can I come?' said **Cat**.
'I can do the sound the engine makes
when it starts to wiggle and jiggle...

PURRR

'Wait for me!' said **Turkey**.
'I can do the sound the tractor makes when it drives off down the lane...

GOBBLE
GOBBLE
GOBBLE

'Let's do it again,' said **Cat**.
'But what about Farmer Dougal?' said **Sheep**.
'What if he wakes up and sees us?'

GOBBLE

Cat and **Turkey** looked at **Sheep**
with two silly smirks and said

P·L·E·A·S·E

'All right,' said **Sheep**.
'Let's go for a ride. READY...

'It's wiggling and jiggling...

PURRRRR

and the tractor is
driving off down the lane...

GOBBLE
GOBBLE
GOBBLE
GOBBLE

'Can I come too?' said Mouse.
'I can do the wheels!
The great big wheels
which go round and round
with a...

SQUEAK SQUEAK SQUEAK

'Wait for me!' said **Goose**. 'I can do the horn, which shouts, "Get out of the way!" with a...

Honk Honk Honk

'I can do the engine when the tractor goes fast,' said **Cow**.
'It gets louder and louder
and sounds like this...

MoooOOOOO!

'Let's do it again!' said Cat.
'We can all join in,' said Mouse.

'But what about Farmer Dougal?' said **Sheep**.

Then **Cat**, **Turkey**, Mouse, **Goose** and **Cow**
looked at **Sheep** with five soppy smiles and said...

P·L·E·A·S·E

'All right,' said **Sheep**. 'Ready...

But then...

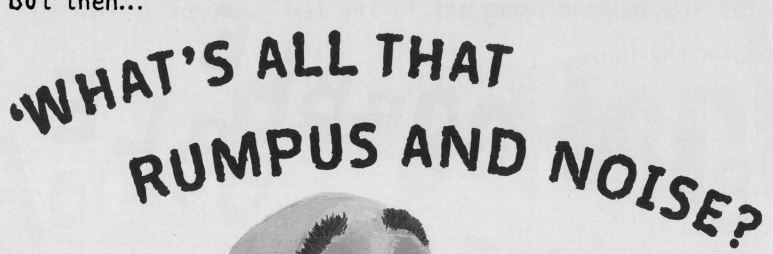

SOMEONE IS DRIVING OFF WITH MY TRACTOR!'

'QUICK!' cried **Sheep**. 'It's Farmer Dougal...

Farmer Dougal looked out of the window...
and there was his big red tractor, safe and sound.

'I must have been dreaming,' he said.
Then he pulled the curtains shut and climbed
back into bed.

Then **Cow** looked at **Sheep**,

Turkey looked at **Sheep**.

Mouse looked at **Sheep**,